3 4028 07744 3175
HARRIS COUNTY PUBLIC LIBRARY

JPIC Franco
Franc
Doub
ar   W9-BYJ-398

DISCARDED

$18.99
ocn651153671
1st ed.   07/26/2011

For Denise. —B.F.
To Ann Bevins. —D.C.

Text copyright © 2011 by Betsy Franco
Illustrations copyright © 2011 by Doug Cushman

All rights reserved. Published in the United States by Tricycle Press, an imprint of Random House Children's Books,
a division of Random House, Inc., New York.
www.randomhouse.com/kids

Tricycle Press and the Tricycle Press colophon are registered trademarks of Random House, Inc.

Library of Congress Cataloging-in-Publication Data
Franco, Betsy.
Double play / by Betsy Franco; illustrations by Doug Cushman.
p. cm.
Summary: Monkey friends Jill and Jake play together at recess, and each game they play provides practice in doubling.
Each page displays the matching addition problem.
[1. Stories in rhyme. 2. Play—Fiction. 3. Recess—Fiction. 4. Monkeys—Fiction. 5. Schools—Fiction. 6. Addition.]
I. Cushman, Doug, ill. II. Title.
PZ8.3.F84765Dou 2011
[E]—dc22
2010024347

ISBN 978-1-58246-384-1 (hardcover)
ISBN 978-1-58246-396-4 (Gibraltar lib. bdg.)

Printed in Malaysia

Design by Betsy Stromberg and Toni Tajima
Typeset in Ed Gothic
The illustrations in this book were rendered in watercolor.

1 2 3 4 5 6 – 16 15 14 13 12 11

First Edition

Double Play!

MONKEYING AROUND WITH ADDITION

by Betsy Franco
Illustrations by Doug Cushman

TRICYCLE PRESS
Berkeley

Br-iiing,
the bell for recess time!
The kids can
gallop,
race,
and climb.

Jill and Jake
line up in twos.
They peek outside.
What will they choose?

1 friend + 1 friend = 2 friends

With just their knees,
they grip the bars.
They're upside-downside
circus stars.

2 knees + 2 knees = 4 knees

Their jumping makes
a rhythmic sound,
while friends turn ropes
that slap the ground.

3 kids + 3 kids = 6 kids

They punch the ball
and make it fly—
from square to square,
b-bouncing high.

4 squares + **4** squares = **8** squares

It's time to eat
a juicy treat.
The grapes they share
are sour 'n sweet.

5 grapes + 5 grapes = 10 grapes

Then pull by pull
and knot by knot,
they make it to
the tippy top.

6 knots + **6** knots = **12** knots

With great big wands,
they dip and blow,
then watch the floating
bubbles glow.

7 bubbles + 7 bubbles = 14 bubbles

Their silly monsters
flap and fly,
and hers have
goofy googly eyes.

The Monster Wall

8 monsters + 8 monsters = 16 monsters

They join a team
and kick and race,
then zoom around
to every base.

9 players + 9 players = 18 players

They climb, they cling.
They swing and glide
until they reach
the other side.

10 bars + **10** bars = **20** bars

Br-iiing,
the bell!
It's time to stop,
so Jill and Jake let go
and drop.

They stand together
by the door.
They're 1 + 1,
just like before!

Harris County Public Library
Houston, Texas